My views and ideas in form of brief essays

ALPESH MARU

© **Alpesh Maru 2019**

All rights reserved

All rights reserved by author. No part of this publication may be reproduced, stored in a retrieval system or transmitted in any form or by any means, electronic, mechanical, photocopying, recording or otherwise, without the prior permission of the author.

Although every precaution has been taken to verify the accuracy of the information contained herein, the author and publisher assume no responsibility for any errors or omissions. No liability is assumed for damages that may result from the use of information contained within.

First Published in October 2019

ISBN: 978-93-5347-875-9

BLUEROSE PUBLISHERS
www.bluerosepublishers.com
info@bluerosepublishers.com
+91 8882 898 898

Cover Design:
Deepak Lal

Typographic Design:
Teena Maurya

Distributed by: Blue Rose, Amazon, Flipkart, Shopclues

Preface

Everything starts with a small idea or intention to do something creative, something novel. If we look back in time then our ancestor started communicating with each other and created a system that we today recognize as language. This system of communication become more and more advanced day by day and as you are reading this book, there will be millions and billions of ideas forming shape of language in the form of the word or definition or a totally new concept.

In this book, we will take a journey into lots of topics that we encounter in our day to day life. For example, you are watching television in your drawing room and suddenly an advertisement left you with an idea to travel to an adventurous place. Suddenly, you started daydreaming about it. You planned your journey to this unknown place and started thinking about the pros and cons of it.

After evaluating everything you came to the conclusion that you will get more benefits by travelling to this place and you made up your mind to go to this place. If you write down all the details that you thought before deciding to go to an adventures place then it will take the form of an article or essay of your opinion about visiting an adventurous place.

In this book, we will discuss about a similar type of fascinating and interesting topics that will leave you with lots of thoughtful ideas. At the end of every topic, I will give my opinion on that topic. So, enjoy this journey!

At the end of the day, I would like to thanks all my family members, tutors and friends who have supported and motivated me through thick and thin.

-Alpesh Maru

*Dedicated to
all divine spirits and well-wishers*

Contents

Topic 1 : How To Make Decisions ? / 1
Topic 2 : Which Is Better Competition Or Collaboration ? / 4
Topic 3 : Why It Is Better To Have More Than One Career Options ? / 8
Topic 4 : Which method of learning is appropriate ? / 11
Topic 5 : Influence of parents and teacher on one's life / 14
Topic 6 : Is living at different place during childhood makes any difference ? / 17
Topic 7 : Importance of language in our life / 20
Topic 8 : What Is the Difference Between Online And Classroom Learning ? / 23
Topic 9 : Importance of Printed Books And Digital books / 26
Topic 10 : Impact Of Taking Part In Extra-curricular Activities / 29
Topic 11 : How Schools Can Impart Good Habits ? / 32
Topic 12 : Increasing Average Weight And Decrease In Level Of Health And Fitness / 35
Topic 13 : Are Imposing Strict Rules Can Kill Creativity ? / 38
Topic 14 : Impact Of Education On Real Life / 41
Topic 15 : How Education Can Help To Reduce Crime Rate ? / 45
Topic 16 : How To Decrease Crime Rate Among Teenagers ? / 49
Topic 17 : Is Past History Of Criminal Matters ? / 53
Topic 18 : How To Ensure Road Safety / 56
Topic 19 : Children Should Leave Family Or Stay At Home / 59
Topic 20 : Why People Stay Away From Home ? / 62
Topic 21 : Pros And Cons Of Part-time Jobs / 66
Topic 22 : Importance Of Interpersonal Skills In Business World /69
Topic 23 : How Employees Can Adapt To Changes In Work Environment ? / 73
Topic 24 : People Working From Home And Working In Offices / 77
Topic 25 : The Mystery Of An Unemployment / 80

Topic 26 : Is Working In A Same Company Is Beneficial ? / 83
Topic 27 : How To Teach Children About Money Related Matters ? / 86
Topic 28 : Is Digital Money Will Completely Replace Paper Money ? / 89
Topic 29 : Is Expenditure On Beauty Product Is Justifiable ? / 92
Topic 30 : New Era Of Online Shopping / 95
Topic 31 : Is Increasing In Shopping Is Good Or Bad ? / 98
Topic 32 : Pros And Cons Of Far Away Shops / 101
Topic 33 : Who Must Handle The Distribution Of Land ? / 104
Topic 34 : Is Public Transportation Should Be Completely Free ? / 107
Topic 35 : Importance Of An Old Buildings / 110
Topic 36 : Is Beauty Matters In Construction Of Buildings ? / 113
Topic 37 : Is Freedom Of Speech Is Required In Society ? / 116
Topic 38 : The Problems Faced By Countries Hosting International Sports Event / 120
Topic 39 : What Is the Difference Between Men Sports And Women Sports? / 124
Topic 40 : Importance Of Digital And Physical Games / 128
Topic 41 : Why Grand Parents Are Best Care Takers ? / 131
Topic 42 : How To Take Care Of Our Elders ? / 134
Topic 43 : Role Of Younger And Older People In Growth Of A Nation / 137
Topic 44 : Working After Retirement / 140
Topic 45 : Rise In Number Of Old People / 143
Topic 46 : Is Increasing Trend In Production of Consumer Goods Is Damaging Environment ? / 146
Topic 47 : Is Cleanliness is Responsibility Of An Individual Or Government ? / 149
Topic 48 : How To Preserve Environment ? / 152
Topic 49 : How To Restore Global Climate Changes ? / 155
Topic 50 : How To Control Industrial Pollution ? / 158
Topic 51 : How To Save Diverse Flora And Fauna Of Earth ? / 161
Topic 52 : Is outer space exploration worthy ? / 164
Topic 53 : Do Machine Can Replace Hand Made Work / 168

Topic 54 : Available Natural Resources For Energy Requirement / 171
Topic 55 : Who Is More Popular Scientists Or Politicians ? / 174
Topic 56 : The Dilemma Of Being Celebrity / 178
Topic 57 : Which Is Better Live Concert Or Live Telecast ? / 181
Topic 58 : Is T.V. Advertisements Are Beneficial / 184
Topic 59 : How To Utilize Materials More Effectively ? / 187
Topic 60 : Smartphones Are Advantageous Or Disadvantageous / 190
Topic 61 : The Mystery Of Happiness / 193
Topic 62 : Requirement Of Security In Modern World / 196
Topic 63 : How To Reduce Wastage Of Food ? / 199
Topic 64 : Is It A Good Idea To Explore About Different Cultures ? / 203
Topic 65 : Impact Of Young People Migrating To Urban Areas / 207
Topic 66 : Urban Migration And Its Effects / 210
Topic 67 : Pros And Cons Of International Tourism / 213
Topic 68 : Nowadays travelling Abroad Is Easier / 216

Topic 1 : How To Make Decisions ?

In our routine life, we make lots of decisions that affect or influence our activities. There are few decisions that have long-term consequences so it is always advisable to make such decisions after appropriate thinking.

The simple decisions are easy to make but taking decisions after broad thinking is a good habit. For example, if a person wants to buy a home then he/she have to decide about the location, facilities and price range before coming to any conclusion. In this case, a quick decision can lead to an inappropriate choice. So proper thinking and planning can help to make a proper choice.

There are lots of jobs and services which requires critical thinking and person doing that job have to take quick decisions. For example, if a person is deactivating the time-bomb then he/she has to think quickly and also have to work very accurately otherwise bomb can explode so in this type of situations quick and correct decision can save from lots of destruction.

Although taking a decision depends on lots of factors but quick and long - term thinking always leads to a fruitful outcome.

What you think?
Write your opinion on it.

Topic 2 : Which Is Better Competition Or Collaboration ?

Competition must be encouraged between individuals. It motivates them to achieve their targets. The different kind of competitions such as debate, quiz, spell bee helps individuals to improve their skills. It also improves their results. A healthy competition is essential for development. On the other side, individuals who were taught to co-operate instead of competing were more polite and helpful. They develop a sense of unity among their group members. Also, more can be achieved in less time with the help of collaborative work.

The different types of competitions such as debate, general knowledge, dance, music, sports and games help in the development of an individual. For example, in debate and general knowledge competition, individuals are able to explore new ideas and interesting facts. It helps them to improve their IQ and communication skills. Also, healthy competition helps to improve the results of an individual.

On the other side, encouraging cooperation among individual helps them to become more polite and helpful. They develop a sense of unity among their group members. For example, two individuals were told to compete and the other two individuals who were almost similar to the previous one was told to do the project in collaboration. After the completion of the task, a few things were noted down, the individuals who competed with each other were bit upset and was not able to learn anything new but the ones who did the project in collaboration were happy and were able to learn lots of new things.

To recapitulate, healthy competition helps in the development of individuals but in most of the situation co-operative work turns out to be more fruitful.

What you think?
Write your opinion on it.

Topic 3 : Why It Is Better To Have More Than One Career Options ?

Life is very easy in imagination but in real life, there are lots of difficulties we have to face to achieve a successful career. So, it is better to have more than one career option these days. Due to the increase in competition and a decline in employment opportunities we have to face lots of problem in establishing a successful career.

The single career option can help us to be more focus on our work and it helps us to achieve a successful career if we make wise choices. Also, working on a multiple career option requires a more amount of energy and resources which if focused on a single career option then one can achieve a good result. Also, single career option helps to do quality work and encourage us to carry out more specific and in-depth work.

On the other hand, multiple careers option can help us to be on the safer side. It can decrease the rate of failure. For example, a person is good at sports and he is pursuing a career in hotel management. If he is not able to get a job in his/her field then he/she can earn money through sports or other activities based on his/her skills. Thus, having a multiple careers option can come to the rescue in a difficult situation.

In conclusion, there are benefits of single career options but the person must be flexible if the situation is not in his/her favour. He must have another option to pursue his/her career.

What you think?
Write your opinion on it.

Topic 4 : Which method of learning is appropriate ?

The basic concept of all subjects must be clear in the mind of students. The subjects such as science, mathematics, history and languages are basic subjects and help in our day to day life. The basic knowledge of these subjects is helpful to develop essential skills. One must know everything about everything and an expert in his/her field of interest.

General subjects such as science and technology, maths, history and languages must be studied by all students. It helps to clear the basic concept in the mind of students. Also, it helps in our daily life. For example, if they have knowledge about world history then it enhances their travelling experience. Similarly, other subjects such as maths and languages help to calculate and communicate respectively. This knowledge is very important to develop essential skills such as night sky observation and navigation, music, dance and painting. If we take an example of night sky observation then the basic knowledge of science and technology is very useful to know about stars and different constellations.

On the other hand, along with basic knowledge of all subjects, a person must have mastery in his/her subject of interest. If a person have expertise in one subject then he/she knows everything about that subject. For example, if a person is having mastery in cooking then he/she can be the best chef and can gain a reputation as well as money.

To recapitulate, one must be a jack of all and expert of one.

What you think?
Write your opinion on it.

Topic 5 : Influence of parents and teacher on one's life

The development of an individuals depends on two factors nature and nurture. Nature is the personality that they acquire from their parents and his own inclinations and interests. Contrary, nature depends on the surroundings and other factors that play a role in their development. The parents teach them very basic things like walking, talking, etc. The other factors are things that they learn from a tutor and school environment which, further help them in the development.

This initial year of development is very important for children to have a healthy and prosperous life. They learn about every minute thing by either playing with toys or their family members. As they grow up parents provide basic amenities and all other resources to pursue their hobbies. Also, most of the children show themselves as a reflection of their parents.

As children grow, parents feel the needs of systemic education so they send them to the best school in the town. Now as they spend most of their time in school so they have the influence of their teachers and friends. A good teacher leaves a long-lasting impression on children and a good friend becomes the best buddies for life. Good teachers not only give them intellectual knowledge but helps them to cop-up with social problems.

All in all, parents and tutor both play an important role in the development of an individual.

What you think?
Write your opinion on it.

Topic 6 : Is living at different place during childhood makes any difference ?

There are lots of posts and government jobs which requires transferring after a specific time interval. The most important effect of the transferable job is on the children. They have to live at different places during their childhood. It affects their childhood but also provides opportunity to explore new places.

The students whose parents are in the military or any other high-class government services have to live at different places during their childhood. The students have to change their school which affects their academic life. They have to face new problems. For example, the student who got an admission in a new school has to make new friends and have to understand the teaching methodology of a new school. Sometimes students lag behind in their study due to delay in admission. In some cases, children are not able to adjust to a new place and it directly affect their results.

There are a few advantages of a transferrable job. The children are able to explore new places in their childhood. They meet new people and make new friends. It also helps to develop practical knowledge of geography in the mind of children. Often children who spend their childhood at different places develop interests in geography and new spaces.

In conclusion, there are a few advantages of transferable jobs but often a student has to face little problem in adjusting to a new place.

What you think?
Write your opinion on it.

Topic 7 : Importance of language in our life

It is known that in past, our ancestor used to communicate with the help of the different type of symbols and drawings. This symbols and drawings became the base of language development. In different civilization, there was a rise in a different type of languages. Presently, there are lots of well-known languages such as English, French, Sanskrit, Mandarin, Spanish, etc.

Language is an essential part of our day-to-day life. To survive in any region, we must be familiar with the local language. It can help us to find the destination, communicate with locals and know about their lifestyle. If we are not aware of the local language then it can lead us to lots of problems. For example, if we need any resources then we have to communicate with the local people in the local language and if we are not knowing the local language then it can create misunderstanding. Also, it can affect our social life, we won't be able to make friends and we might feel aloof.

In conclusion, there are lots of consequences that we might have to face if we are not able to communicate properly with the help of language.

What you think?
Write your opinion on it.

Topic 8 : What Is the Difference Between Online And Classroom Learning ?

In past, there was no internet or any other facilities which can assist students. The tutor used to explain to their pupils using blackboard and pupils used to learn with the help of slate and chalk. E-book, projector, tablet and internet came later and it has helped the spread of education throughout the globe.

Every student requires a certain amount of time to understand a particular concept and a tutor tries it's best to explain concepts and uses all possible means through which he/she can impart knowledge. Nowadays children are more fascinated with technological gadgets and the internet so most of the students are more comfortable with online lectures. In some case, it helps to strengthen the concepts that already taught by the tutor in the classroom. Also going through the notes before attending any lecture really helps to understand the concept with a better perspective. Students become more curious about the lecture if they already know a little bit about the lecture.

In some case, if the student is absent in the lecture due to some reason then he/she can go through the uploaded online lecture. In some cases, uploading a lecture can create a problem for a lecturer. For example, the student can remain absent in the lecture or they can totally avoid face to face lectures. It can affect their result. Also, the student can become lazy and can lack the benefits of a face to face lecture such as healthy interactions.

The new technology has increased the level of education and it has made learning more fun and exciting.

What you think?
Write your opinion on it.

Topic 9 : Importance of Printed Books And Digital books

Libraries were built to provide space and resources to enhance and preserve knowledge and important information. Library store collection of books which were written by famous authors, researchers, poets, artists and novelists. The digital books can serve as an alternative to printed books. Digital books are user-friendly, eco-friendly and provide more features and functions.

Printed books are tangible and it gives a different feeling to the reader so people prefer to read printed books. Also, it was part of human life for a long time. Nowadays, technological advancements have given us a new alternative in the form of E-books. Digital books are eco - friendly and thus help us to save trees and restore the environment. Digital books can be used as a backup in case of accidental fire or any other natural calamities. Digital books have many features and functions such as an in-built dictionary, highlight, notes and bookmark which makes reading more convenient and easier for the reader.

On the other hand, digital books are dependent on computer system which are prone to virus and malware. Also, the computer system is operated on batteries and it requires a power source. So sometimes it is more convenient to read printed books if we are in a remote location where electricity is not available.

In a nutshell, digital books and printed books both are an important part of the modern world.

**What you think?
Write your opinion on it.**

Topic 10 : Impact Of Taking Part In Extra-curricular Activities

Nowadays in each and every sector, there is cut-throat competition so parents are preparing their children from the very beginning of their childhood. Also, most of the companies are demanding multitalented and dexterous employees.

This is an era of modern technology and the internet. Awareness and knowledge are increasing among the people, also they are becoming smarter. So, parents are motivating their children to learn new skills and to take part in extracurricular activities apart from their regular education. Also, in some cases, parents are enforcing their children to learn more skills due to peer influence and/or social status. For example, some parents oblige their children to join swimming classes because all their friends are going for it.

This tendency can help children to learn lots of skills and they can achieve medal and certificate in his/her field of interest such as sports, music, dance, drama etc. But it can also go wrong. For example, children can become busy in learning new skills so that they are not able to enjoy their childhood. Sometimes, it can lead to stress and children can become victims of overburden.

In short, learning new skills and taking part in extracurricular activities is always helpful but there must be a balance between work and leisure activities.

What you think?
Write your opinion on it.

Topic 11 : How Schools Can Impart Good Habits ?

Schools are concentrating more on regular subjects such as maths, science, languages and social studies. Also, it provides space for sports and other extracurricular activities. The system of education does not have a provision for health-related studies. Providing health-related awareness can help to avoid the spread of diseases.

Health education plays a major role in spreading awareness about diseases. Children are more vulnerable to diseases due to their low immunity. Viral diseases such as polio, chickenpox, etc. Can be prevented by a simple vaccination process. If schools provide awareness about such diseases then it can be prevented. Also, simple information about washing hands, using handkerchiefs while sneezing and other healthy habits can help to prevent diseases.

Schools must provide a special subject on the prevention of diseases. It must incorporate information about health issues and measures to prevent it. This subject can include a description of diseases in the form of a story so that children can understand it in a better manner. Also, schools can organize regular health check-ups. Schools must organize the conference to stop the spread of the epidemic.

To recapitulate, schools must focus on health education along with regular studies.

What you think?
Write your opinion on it.

_____

_____

_____

_____

_____

_____

_____

_____

_____

_____

_____

_____

_____

_____

_____

_____

_____

_____

Topic 12 : Increasing Average Weight And Decrease In Level Of Health And Fitness

The weight of a person depends on lots of factors. The BMI (Body Mass Index) is the unit to measure the weight of a healthy person. BMI provides height to weight ratio to measure the appropriate weight. If the body is not grown homogenously then it can cause health-related problems.

The root cause lies in evolutionary development. In past, our ancestors used to live in extreme conditions. So, our body evolved with a mechanism to store energy in the form of fat. It helped them to survive. Nowadays, we have different conditions than those of the past. We are blessed with lots of food and due to the lazy lifestyle, our weight is increasing day by day.

As we have seen that lazy lifestyle is causing major problem so one solution is to improve our lifestyle. Exercises such as yoga, meditation and cardio workouts can help to achieve appropriate BMI. One can also enrol in sports activities such as cricket, badminton, tennis etc. It helps to lose weight and thus we can become fit.

To recapitulate, there are few factors which cause fitness related problem but by improving our lifestyle and adopting good habits, we can solve this problem.

What you think?
Write your opinion on it.

Topic 13 : Are Imposing Strict Rules Can Kill Creativity ?

Generally, following a set of rules can help to develop discipline in an individual. It plays an important role in developing a personality and a unique identity of teenagers. Also, it helps to preserve our culture and tradition. On the other hand, if young people are allowed to act freely then they develop creativity. It provides a sense of freedom and encourages originality. Also imposing a strict set of rules on teenagers makes them orthodox.

Discipline is very important in shaping the personality of an individual. Discipline can be developed by setting good habits and following a set of rules. This discipline is essential to learn different skills such as music, horse riding, literature etc. It can help a person to complete his/her work on time.

On the other hand, it is important to develop creativity in an individual. If they are allowed to act freely then they create new and novel things. It also creates a sense of freedom in them. Sometimes imposing strict rules on teenagers makes them orthodox and kills their originality.

To recapitulate, imposing a strict set of rules on an individual will help them to develop discipline but sometimes it makes them Orthodox and kills their creativity.

What you think?
Write your opinion on it.

Topic 14 : Impact Of Education On Real Life

In past, people used to live in a forest. Eventually, evolution leads us to a smarter approach. Our ancestor formed a group and started exploring different means of food and adobe. Also, human developed one of the most important means to communicate with each other in the form of language. Language helped us to pass information from one generation to another. It was a big leap in the development of human being and the origin of the essential part of our education. It helped to establish business and another setup to form a developed society. Along with all this development, we also developed materials and tools that caused disruption in the environment.

In order to achieve homogeneous development, we must focus on more practical and skill-oriented knowledge. One of the important factors for it is to incorporate more practical education. The subjects such as science and mathematics can be better understood by practical implementation. For example, the very common and popular molecule in chemistry is water. If a student only remembers its molecular formula (H_2O) and not able to understand its uses and properties then it will be of no use. So, education must consist of a more practical approach.

Science led us to the invention of chemical compounds such as gun powder and other explosives which did lots of destruction in the world wars. Also, the development of nuclear and chemical weapons did lots of destruction in the world wars. The nuclear attack in Hiroshima and

Nagasaki caused health-related issues such as genetic mutation and its radiation changed the genetic make-up of people.

To recapitulate, education leads us to new discoveries and invention. If all this development is applied in proper manners then it can make the world a better place to live.

What you think?
Write your opinion on it.

_____

_____

_____

_____

_____

_____

_____

_____

_____

_____

_____

_____

_____

_____

_____

_____

_____

Topic 15 : How Education Can Help To Reduce Crime Rate ?

Education is really important for imparting moral values and ethics. In history, we can find lots of examples of people who were criminal in the beginning but changed to a good person after getting a good education. Education also helps to direct criminals to good activities which can benefit society. On the other hand, there are many nations which consider punishment such as prison sentence as the ultimate method to reduce crime. Prison sentence is a fruitful mean to provide justice. Also, it helps to create a sense of rehabilitation among criminal.

Presently, education is the best tool for inculcating moral values and ethics among the public. In past, there was a very strict educational system and it was regulated by pope and cardinal. This system helped the ruler to control criminal activities. Criminals were sent to the cathedral for confession and to get an education. With the help of education, a criminal can be converted into a good person. Also, the culprit can be motivated to learn new skills so that he/she can earn and help in the development of society.

On the other hand, there are many nations who believe that a prison sentence is the ultimate option to reduce crime. Prison sentence helps to provide justice. It is important to establish the judiciary system. Also giving a prison sentence helps to create a sense of rehabilitation among criminal. It gives a strong example for those who are doing the crime.

Overall, the prison sentence is effective to create a stable judicial system but education is very important to remove crime from societies.

What you think?
Write your opinion on it.

Topic 16 : How To Decrease Crime Rate Among Teenagers ?

The major reason behind committing any crime is poverty or bad situations that encourage a youngster to do unethical things also nowadays, information about explosives, guns and other weapons are available on the internet, it motivates children to try it out and which lead to crimes. The possible solution is to implement compulsory education for all and provide employment to youngsters. Also, information on the internet must be regulated to stop spread of information that increases the crime rate among the young generation.

If we ask any robber about their past life then he/she will most likely to state poverty as the main reason for becoming a robber. As per the survey was done by the police department, poverty is the main reason behind the increasing crime rate among the young generation. Also, nowadays, everything is available on the internet and youngster are spending more time on it. They have all the information to make harmful explosive and guns and it leads them to accidental crimes. For example, as per published newspaper article, one child accidently killed his friend while playing with explosive material that he made by watching video on YouTube.

The solution is very simple, to decrease the crime rate among youngster, the government must implement compulsory education and provide employment to poor people. Also, information available on the internet must be strictly regulated by search engines. Parents can use software such as quick heal to block harmful websites and to monitor activities of their kids.

In conclusion, the main reason behind the increasing crime rate among youngster is poverty and information available on the internet. The solution is to provide education and employment to poor people and regulate information on the internet.

What you think?
Write your opinion on it.

Topic 17 : Is Past History Of Criminal Matters ?

The present law about the nondisclosure of criminal's information and his/her past criminal record is established to ensure the privacy of a criminal. This law is established to avoid any biasing. As per the suggestion of a lawyer in some cases, there are chances that a criminal's past record can help the jury to give a proper judgement.

The personal information of any criminal must not be revealed. The personal information of a criminal is not helpful in the case. It only diverts the case. Revealing personal information to the jury creates an impression of a criminal which can affect the final judgment. For example, if the criminal is a relative of any jury member then this personal information of a criminal can crowd the judgement of a jury member. Also, these facts can put the jury members into a dilemma and it can affect the final decision.

On the other hand, giving the past facts of a criminal to the jury can help the lawyer to create an impression of criminal and it helps him/her in the case. Sometimes this fact can change the whole scenario of the case. For example, if the criminal is suffering from the disorder such as split personality then such type of facts can help the jury to come to the conclusion.

In conclusion, there are very few situations in which personal information of a criminal can help a jury so it is advisable not to reveal the personal information to the jury if it is not related to the case.

What you think?
Write your opinion on it.

Topic 18 : How To Ensure Road Safety ?

Traffic rules are formed to avoid accidents. The general public must follow them. If someone breaks the rule then his/her mistake can cause an accident. Punishment can help to establish awareness among the public. On the other hand, the government can improve the road system and they can use the latest technologies to increase road safety.

Mostly teenagers break the traffic rules and they are careless. Punishment can decrease driving offences to some extent but it is the responsibility of people to take care while driving an automobile. In some cases, the innocent has to suffer due to reckless driving. For example, if a person was drunk and encounter collision with an incoming car then people who were sitting in the car has to suffer due to the mistake of a drunk driver.

The solution is to implement technologies to create smart roads. For example, with the help of Artificial Intelligence and machine learning, a road system can be created so that it can help the driver to avoid a collision. Also, driverless cars and other safety systems such as airbags, suspension and advanced braking play an important role in reducing casualties.

All in all, traffic rules are important to some extent but to reduce road accidents smart technologies must be introduced in existing road systems.

What you think?
Write your opinion on it.

Topic 19 : Children Should Leave Family Or Stay At Home

Children are having the fastest rate of growth. If children leave the house in his/her early childhood then there are lots of benefits such as individual personality development, learn new skills to cope up with developing the environment and he/she gets ample of time to work on himself/herself. On the other hand, staying with family members has its own perks such as family bonding, family care and happiness.

As childhood is the most important part of anyone's life, it must be designed in such a manner so that it can help to shape his/her personality. If children leave home in his/her early childhood then he/she can spend his/her time on developing new skills, learning new things which can help him/her to live a happy & independent life.

Contrary, if a child decides to stay with his/her parents then there are lots of benefits such as family bonding, family care and comfy and happy environment. Family bonding plays an important role in the development of children. The humid and comfy environment of the house helps to develop empathy in children. Also, parents can provide essential resources for the intellectual development of children. In the case of any medical problems, no one can take care better than that of parents so staying with parents is the best option for children with congenital diseases.

All in all, no doubt leaving home in early childhood have its own benefits but staying with family members can provide emotional as well as intellectual development.

What you think?
Write your opinion on it.

Topic 20 : Why People Stay Away From Home ?

There are many reasons such as study, jobs or work, exploration due to which people spend less time at their home. Most of the people go out for study purposes, it helps them to develop individually but sometimes they come in contact with bad influence. Also, people go out for job/work, it helps them to earn money. Nowadays due to globalization, most people spend their time in exploration. Explorer is happier than any other people. Also, exploration helps to discover new places and cultures which helps to unite two different civilization.

Most people go out for study purposes. It is really important for individual development. People gain new knowledge and learn new skills. It helps them to get a good job and a handsome salary. Also, people stay away from their adobe for a job or work, they become prosperous and live an extravagant life but sometimes they come in contact with bad influence. It diverts their attention and leads to criminal activities. Due to which society and individual faces huge loss. Nowadays crime such as robbery, murder is increasing and it creates instability in society.

People also stay away from their adobe for the purpose of exploring new places. Due to globalization, transportation facilities are increased. Nowadays we have cruise, aeroplane and other means of transportation. These facilities aid exploration and provide ease and comfort. Exploration is important to discover new places and cultures. This exploration works as a bridge between two different civilization. It helps in the development of society and create employment opportunities.

There are many reasons such as study, jobs, expeditions, etc due to which people away from home and it helps in the development of society and individual.

What you think?
Write your opinion on it.

Topic 21 : Pros And Cons Of Part-time Jobs

Teenage is the most important stage of human life. In teenage, we become more aware of our surroundings and ongoing life. Most of the country promote teenagers to do part-time jobs. Also, there are a few successful personalities who started earning from their teenage. While there are some governments who have an opinion that teenagers must concentrate on their studies.

In teenage, most of the students are very energetic and have a flexible mindset so doing part-time jobs really helps them to learn new skills. Also doing part-time job he/she can earn money. For example, if a student is not having a good financial condition and he/she is very good in the study then the part-time job can become a boon for him/her. On the other hand, few part-time jobs provide other facilities such as transportation expenses, a free meal, discount coupons etc.

Some country encourages the teenager to concentrate more on their study rather than doing part-time job. As part-time job can affect one's study due to time constraints. For example, if one is spending more time in his/her part-time job then he/she will not be able to spend more time to study and it can severely affect his/her grades. Also, part-time job can be stressful and teenagers can feel overburden.

In conclusion, no doubt there is some downside of part-time jobs but most of the teenagers get lots of benefits from part-time jobs.

What you think?
Write your opinion on it.

Topic 22 : Importance Of Interpersonal Skills In Business World

There is a vast difference between the environment of college and industry. Most of the colleges provide resources for the study purposes and students are more concern about their exams. So, throughout the year, they prepare for their exams. They give more focus on theoretical subjects and give less time to practical skills. So, one of the solutions is to give more emphasis on skills that can be helpful in real life.

The education system of most of the colleges is more focused on quantity then that of quality. This type of approach leads to an imbalance between theoretical and practical studies. Also due to the burden of learning multiple subjects in very less time, students are not able to acquire interpersonal skills that can come handy in real life. Most of the industries look for employees who are dexterous. Multi-tasking, communication skills and other talents can help them to get a good job.

The solution is to update an education system by designing a balanced syllabus which can incorporate both practical as well as theoretical studies. More focus must be given on quality education rather than on quantity. Also, colleges must have a collaboration with industries so that student can learn more about the industrial environment. The student must be encouraged to take part in an internship. It can help them to learn skills which is essential to get a good job.

To recapitulate, the bridge between college life and professional life can be constructed by encouraging the student to acquire skills that are essential in real life.

What you think?
Write your opinion on it.

Topic 23 : How Employees Can Adapt To Changes In Work Environment ?

With the rise in industrialization, privatization and globalization, the new work market has emerged. The machines, computer software and internet has changed the way people work. The new job opportunities are created along with a dynamic work environment. This new work culture requires less labour work and more smart work.

In the past, most of the people were depended on farming or another sort of labour work but with the invention of the new machine and other emerging technologies the working environment has changed. With the new emerging technologies and machines, there is a huge requirement of people with skills to handle this new equipment. With the technological revolution, the working environment is becoming more dynamic. The new emerging jobs require skills and qualification to cope up with the changing work environment. Lots of people get habituated to their working environment and resist any change in their working conditions. These people can't survive in new working conditions. They have to develop plasticity with new evolving working conditions.

The best way is to train them from the very beginning of their college life. The students must be trained to evolve with dynamic working conditions. The existing employees must be trained with the help of workshops and other training sessions to develop an aptitude to co-up with dynamic working conditions.

In conclusion, I would like to mention that there is always resistance and difficulties with new changes but one must learn to adopt it.

What you think?
Write your opinion on it.

Topic 24 : People Working From Home And Working In Offices

Working from home is always an interesting idea for employees and students. It can increase the productivity of employees and of the company for whom they are working. For students, computer technology can enhance their learning experience. On the other hand, employees will get less experience of fieldwork. The employees working from their adobe will become lazy and it can affect their overall health.

Most of the employees spend their time in grooming and travelling to the office. This activity consumes lots of time and decreases their productivity. As per the survey was done by a media house, people who work from their home are more productive compared to employees working at the office. Computer technologies can enhance the learning experience of students with the help of audio-visual aid. Researchers have proved that computer-aided education is more effective than any other methods.

On the other hand, people working from their home will become lazy and it will raise health-related concerns. As per the paper published in a research journal, people working from their home are more likely to get physical problems such as obesity. Also, employees will get less experience in fieldwork.

In conclusion, no doubt there are few health-related concerns but apart from that working from home is considered as one of the best options for employees as well as students. Also, the quality of work matters whether he/she is working at home/office.

What you think?
Write your opinion on it.

Topic 25 : The Mystery Of An Unemployment

There is a vast difference in school and job environment which create a need to establish a bridge between it. The education system put more emphasis on theoretical knowledge and it creates an imbalance between theoretical and practical studies. So proper steps must be taken to improve education and to establish a skill-oriented education system.

The environment of the school is very different from that of industries. So, students lack essential skills that are required for obtaining a good job. Also, due to increasing pollution, there is a rise in competition. To survive in this world, one has to be more dextrous and versatile. Apart from all this factor, there is a rising concern about corruption in the government sector, due to corruption, the system gets corrugated and it leads to unemployment.

First and foremost, school must do a tie-up with industries and give more focus on skill-oriented education. Also, the student must be encouraged to take part in sports activities so that they can pursue their careers in it. Lastly, the government must take a proper step to create employment and to eradicate corruption from a system.

All in all, there are lots of factors that lead to unemployment so proper steps must be taken to create new opportunities.

What you think?
Write your opinion on it.

Topic 26 : Is Working In A Same Company Is Beneficial ?

It is good to work in a same company for a very long time. Firstly, it shows loyalty and there is a greater chance of promotion. Secondly, working in the same organization can give a steady career. On the other hand, there is a chance of getting a better salary if we change the company.

Conventional people think that it is good to stick with one company because of its lead to a stable career. Also, there are more chances of getting a promotion. For example, two friends were working in the same company. Both of them was very loyal to his company and others were interested in exploring new companies. Eventually, the one who was loyal got promoted and become a general manager of a company.

On the other hand, exploring new companies can help to get a better salary. Also, a person can get new experience by doing different types of jobs in different companies. The person who is interested in travelling would be more likely to change his/her company. As different companies are located at different locations.

To recapitulate, the person who sticks to his/her company is more likely to get a promotion.

What you think?
Write your opinion on it.

Topic 27 : How To Teach Children About Money Related Matters ?

In the world run with the help of an economic system, it is very important to have knowledge about money and its different functions. The monetary system is very old. With the development of different civilizations, the monetary system gets updated and become more effective.

As the monetary system is an essential part of our life. It is very important for children to learn to use it judicially. Nowadays new technologies are emerging and children are getting more interested in all those technologies so learning how to spend their pocket money will help them to avoid unnecessary purchases.

The primary knowledge about the money and how the system works can be taught to children by showing him/her a documentary or infotainment videos but to give him/ her a practical taste the parents can guide him/her to sell a small object or any goods and the experience gained by that event will really help him/her to understand the practical aspect of money.

In conclusion, knowledge about money and how it matters to us must be given to children.

What you think?
Write your opinion on it.

_____

_____

_____

_____

_____

_____

_____

_____

_____

_____

_____

_____

_____

_____

_____

_____

_____

_____

Topic 28 : Is Digital Money Will Completely Replace Paper Money ?

Paper money and coins are basic systems that are designed in order to carry out financial transactions. Nowadays with advancement in technology, we have better alternative of paper money and coins in form of digital money. Paper money and coins have downsides such as it is tangible, creates workload and corruption. On the other side, the digital payment method is more effective, transparent, easy and convenient.

Paper money and coins were designed during the period of the monarchy. It is a very old system of carrying out financial transactions. Paper money and coins are tangible means of exchanging goods. So, it can be destructed or imitated by anyone. Paper money and coins also increase workload and people have to stand in line in order to carry out monetary transactions.

Digital payment methods are more effective than that of paper money and coins. Digital money has its own perks. It provides transparency in all the monetary transactions. Digital money is intangible so there is no problem of destruction or imitation. People don't have to stand in line in order to carry out simple transactions. With the help of digital payment method, people can carry out simple transactions with the help of a mobile phone.

As per my opinion, in the near future, there will be a museum of a collection of paper money and coins which will be having visitors and donors doing payment using digital transactions.

What you think?
Write your opinion on it.

Topic 29 : Is Expenditure On Beauty Product Is Justifiable ?

The money spend on cosmetics is much more than that of other sectors such as food, shelter and other necessary resources. Due to the development of science, there are lots of cosmetic product available in the market. These products are really helpful in the establishment of cosmetic industries, on the other hand, poor people are in need of food and shelter. So, some part of the money must be utilized in the development of poor people.

Poverty is a major problem in our country. Lots of people live in raw houses and streets. Some people even find it difficult to earn a two-time meal. So, the money spent on cosmetic and other beauty products must be utilized in providing a better shelter and food facility to the poor and needy people.

The cosmetic industry generates lots of employment and revenue. The cosmetic and other beauty product help to provide employment. Also, it helps the Bollywood industry to generate revenue. The celebrity is the main consumer of beauty products. So, it helps to provide employment and to provide employment and to generate revenue.

All in all, cosmetic and other beauty product must be used and manufactured in a moderate amount and money must be spent on the development of poor and needy people.

What you think?
Write your opinion on it.

Topic 30 : New Era Of Online Shopping

Online shopping is a new and trending concept. It became very popular in the last few years. There are lots of benefits that attract new customers. It provides lots of varieties. On the other side, there is a risk of fraud and other disadvantages which creates ambiguity in the buyer's mind.

Shopping is very popular among people and it creates lots of revenue. The textile industries play a major role in the development of the country. With the rise in information technology, lots of company came up with online shopping websites. These websites have gained popularity in a very short time. It provides a large range of varieties in the selection of clothes. It provides home delivery and a various method of payment including net banking, cash on delivery, online wallet etc. Also, it provides handsome discounts on festivals.

There are a few downsides of online shopping. Online shopping websites provide images of fabric and buyer have to select it by assuming material and quality. Also, some cases of online shopping fraud became popular in media. Customers reported that they got low-quality materials than that of shown on the website. It leads to the atmosphere of distrust among online shopping.

In conclusion, online shopping must be regulated by the proper system to ensure quality and customer satisfaction.

What you think?
Write your opinion on it.

Topic 31 : Is Increasing In Shopping Is Good Or Bad ?

In past, people have to face lots of problems due to scarcity of things that are essential in our day to day life but nowadays due to technological advancement, we have lots of options. The online website such as Amazon provides all kind of household goods with handsome discounts. This development has raised the standard of living. Also, we get energy-efficient and better-quality equipment. On the other hand, this development has resulted in the overexploitation of natural resources and due to which the entire world is facing environmental problems.

Technological advancement leads to the development of e-commerce websites such as Amazon, Flipkart, Olx, Ajio, etc. Amazon provides lots of options for all kind of household items. Amazon is having its own wallet for payment and it provides huge discounts to the customers. As it is online, we can purchase anything from anywhere, the only thing we need is a smartphone and internet connection. All this development has raised our standard of living.

On the other hand, all this development has caused overexploitation of natural resources and due to which we are facing environmental problems such as global warming, air and water pollution, scarcity of fossil fuel. Also, natural disasters such as earthquakes, tsunami, storms are increasing day by day.

To recapitulate, this development has lots of positive impacts on our life, it has raised our standard of living but due to overexploitation of natural resources, we are facing lots of environmental problems.

What you think?
Write your opinion on it.

Topic 32 : Pros And Cons Of Far Away Shops

Nowadays due to urbanization and town development, we are moving toward more organized cities and towns. Designed and planned cities provide better infrastructure and environment for living. It also helps to reduce noise, as well as light pollution, creating shops outside of town, provides good space and a clean environment to live. On the other side, people have to travel more to purchase and buy goods. As shops are far from the city centre, car and transportation expenses rises.

Urbanization leads to the development of new towns and megacities. Nowadays, we find better-organized cities and towns. It provides the best infrastructure and qualitative environment for living. As shops are outside of town, it provides good space to create residential buildings and other amenities. Also, as shops are outside of town, it reduces the density of a place and which in turn reduces noise as well as light pollution.

If we look at another side, development of outside shops leads to lots of inconveniences. As shops are far from the residential area, people have to travel more distance to purchase and buy goods. Also, as shops are far from the city centre, car and transportation expense increases. People have to spend more money on car and public transportation.

To recapitulate, the development of more outside shops helps to keep the city well-organized and well-maintained with few public inconveniences.

What you think?
Write your opinion on it.

Topic 33 : Who Must Handle The Distribution Of Land ?

In the past, the ruler of any reign used to handle the distribution of land to have a dispute free environment and also to carry out the development of his/her region. So, from the very beginning of civilization, the distribution of land and another construction-related aspect is controlled by the ruling government.

The design and layout of any building are constructed by the engineer while the building is constructed by the contractors and construction workers. The design of a building affects the financial outcomes so it is necessary that it must be regulated by the government. Also, the design of a building can influence the city. For example, if the building is to be constructed in the centre or in highly-populated areas then it can influence the traffic and can cause a problem to the public.

If the government or the design approving body is too strict then it can cause a problem for the owner or the contractor who wants to construct a building. Usually, the contractor spends lots of money to make building more functional and to provide a good facility to the civilians so some freedom must be there for the design of buildings.

In my opinion, moderate regulation of building and other construction must be there.

What you think?
Write your opinion on it.

Topic 34 : Is Public Transportation Should Be Completely Free ?

If public transportation is made free of cost then there will be degradation in the quality of buses and the overall transportation system. Also, the cost of maintenance will increase. On the other hand, poor people and students can benefit from free transportation.

If public transportation is made free of cost then more and more people will use public transportation facilities. It will decrease the quality of buses and people will suffer from suffocation due to crowded buses. Also, the government will have to spend more money on maintenance of the transportation system, it will increase the burden of government. As per the survey done by a local newspaper, If the public transportation system is made free of cost then it will negatively affect the transportation system.

On the other hand, the only people who will benefit from free public transportation are poor people and students. Poor people don't have much money to spend on transportation and it affects their employment as they reach late to their work area. Also, the student has limited pocket money so they can do the saving by using free public transportation.

To recapitulate, there are benefits as well as disadvantages of providing completely free public transportation.

What you think?
Write your opinion on it.

Topic 35 : Importance Of An Old Buildings

Old buildings must be preserved. It is built by our ancestors who used to rule the respective province. It has historical importance. Also, archaeologist studies these buildings and carry out research on it. Contrary, constructing new adobe and pathways require a huge amount of resources and manpower. Also, it requires a huge amount of time.

Renovation of old buildings is an easy task compared to the construction of a new building. Also preserving this old building can help to boost the economy. Old buildings are always the centre of attraction for tourist. Specially forts and another historical monument. Revenue generated from tourism can help in the development of the city. Also, old buildings can be used as government offices.

On the other hand, building new adobe and pathways requires a huge amount of resources. Also, it takes time in constructing a new building. The benefits are that it can be used to allocate houses for poor people and new roads can solve the traffic problem. Also constructing a new building can help to improve the architecture along with new facilities and technological advancement which can be incorporated in a new building.

All in all, there are benefits of constructing a new building but the restoration of an old building is a better option.

What you think?
Write your opinion on it.

Topic 36 : Is Beauty Matters In Construction Of Buildings ?

Aesthetics and comfort are the two main feature of any building. Outer appearance attracts customers to buy a space, on the other hand, good facilities ensure the comfort of a buyer. Most of the architect focus on the comfort of the building because it is the basic and necessary requirement.

The purpose of any building or construction varies as per the requirements. The purpose of the building includes its facilities and technological advancement that is used to construct it. Most of the high-rise building is constructed for the purpose of providing adobe or for the purpose of providing adobe or for business purposes. The building constructed for the dwelling includes facilities such as garden, parking, apartments with well-furnished furniture. The building constructed for business includes big shops and cinema halls. There are few buildings constructed for social events such as marriage and family celebrations.

Aesthetic of any building attract tourists. Also, beautiful buildings become a spot for outings such as beautiful forts and other historical monuments. It increases tourism. Also, a few architects gain rewards and fame by constructing beautiful buildings.

All in all, aesthetic is important but the architecture must focus on the purpose of the building.

What you think?
Write your opinion on it.

Topic 37 : Is Freedom Of Speech Is Required In Society ?

Freedom of speech is very important in the present scenario. In the present world, most of the countries are democratic. It is run by publicly elected representatives and ministers so freedom of speech become common means to establish transparency between government and public. Positive feedback always helps to correct the mistake and to establish a trustworthy relationship. Freedom of speech is an essential right to advocate our own opinion. Also, it helps to find a solution to existing problems by means of debates. Contrary, sometimes freedom of speech can create chaos and riots. It must be used wisely to avoid problems.

Freedom of speech is essential and become common in modern world. It helps to create a transparent relation among the government and public. Presently, media and other means of communication play an important role in creating connection between people. Freedom of speech is important for solving problems by means of debate. Nowadays ample of debates are carried out on global issues such as global warming, wildlife conservation, population and other major issues.

Contrary, if freedom of speech is not used wisely then it can create lots of problems. A controversial statement from any influential leader can provoke the public to create a riot and bring the threat to life and public resources. Similarly, if a sensitive information is leaked then it can create major problems or can lead to war.

All in all, freedom of speech is very important in modern world but if it is not used wisely can lead to major problems.

What you think?
Write your opinion on it.

Topic 38 : The Problems Faced By Countries Hosting International Sports Event

International sporting events started way back before the 19th century. It includes the involvement of different countries. The main focus of such types of event is to develop a good relationship between the neighbouring countries. Also, it helps to boost the economy of the organizing country. International sporting events are a very effective means of increasing tourism. Lastly, the health benefits can't be ignored. Contrary, the organizing country have to build-up huge infrastructures and have to maintain it. Also, there is a risk of the rampage, chaos, and another security-related problem.

International sporting events are the best way to establish a friendly relation with the neighbouring countries. The organizing country has ample of benefits. The most important one is the increase in tourism. As these types of event are organized considering a huge amount of crowd. The organizing country is benefited directly by the revenue generated from the visitors, fans and cheering crowd. Ultimately, as the organizing country is also participating in the sporting event, there is a good chance of winning of the host nation. lastly, sporting events encourage exercise and a healthy lifestyle so it is beneficial for the local public who are encouraged and motivated by such types of events.

Contrary, International sporting events comes with ample of responsibility. The organizing country has to build-up huge infrastructures and has to maintain it. Construction of these types of infrastructures require lots of revenues and manpower. Also, these types of event are having lots of security issues. As it is organized on a bigger platform, there are chances of chaos, rampage and other security related problems. So proper arrangement has to be done before the inauguration of international sporting events.

To recapitulate, international sporting events comes with both development and risk. So proper management is required for success of an event.

What you think?
Write your opinion on it.

Topic 39 : What Is the Difference Between Men Sports And Women Sports?

From the very beginning of civilization, men were interested in outdoor activities such as hunting. They used to carry out hunting and had a responsibility to bring food at home on the other hand women used to take care of their children and carry out other household activities. Men started exploring different types of sports activities and presently, there are lots of sports activities out there. Also, they have mastered all these sports activities due to practice and past experience. Nowadays women are also taking part in sports activities and it is a positive development. As sports helps to develop physical and mental strength it is advisable that both men and women take part in sports activities.

The major reason for the dominance of men in International sports activities is evolution. Men were always involved in outdoor activities while women used to take care of children and other household activities. Men used to go out in woods and used to do hunting and other activities for survival. Another factor is time, women used to be busy in her day to day activities and were not able to take part in outdoor activities.

Presently, the scenario is changing. The world is moving toward gender equality and men and women are both taking part in each and every activity. World's best chefs are men and women are showing outstanding performance in international sports. So clearly, men and women are taking part in activities based on their interests and skills.

Thus, in my opinion, equal attention must be given to both men and women sports.

To recapitulate, as per the present scenario men, as well as women sports, must be given equal importance.

What you think?
Write your opinion on it.

Topic 40 : Importance Of Digital And Physical Games

Urbanization and technological development are major factors of change in lifestyle. The world of the video game is advancing day by day. The gaming platform such as Xbox and play station are very famous among children. Smartphones are becoming more popular among all age group. All these technological gadgets are affecting the lifestyle of younger people. The solution is to encourage them to take part in sports and other outdoor activities.

The lifestyle of each and every people is changing due to advancement in technology. Due to T.V and video games, they spend most of their time playing virtual games and watching T.V. In a science research, group of scientists have coined a term couch potato for people spend most of their time in playing video games. All these passive activities create health-related problems such as obesity and other disorders. Also, education is affected due to all these activities.

The solution is to encourage them to take part in outdoor activities such as playing sports. The outdoor sports such as cricket, hockey and tennis are popular. Also, meditation and exercise can improve health. The other way is to focus on healthy habits such as night sky watching, playing a musical instrument, etc.

All in all, both digital as well as physical games are an important part of a healthy lifestyle.

What you think?
Write your opinion on it.

Topic 41 : Why Grand Parents Are Best Care Takers ?

Nowadays lifestyle is becoming more hectic and parents are working throughout the day, so most of the parents rely on grandparents to take care of their children. There are lots of benefits and also a few disadvantages.

In most of the families, both parents work to secure the future of their children. So, they often rely on grandparents to take care of their children. In this way, they are satisfied that their children are in good hands and they can concentrate on their work without worrying about their children. Also, grandparents can impart their wisdom and can help their grandchildren to develop a good moral character. Grandparents can help them to complete their homework and can help them to understand difficult topics which can improve their academic record.

The major disadvantage is the generation gap which can cause a problem. For example, if children are smart and tech-savvy then they will be using more technical gadgets and generally, grandparents are not used to with most of the advanced technological gadgets so it can create a problem. Also, in old age, there are lots of health related problems which can affect their dexterity.

In conclusion, grandparents are the best caretakers and the children who get such an opportunity are fortunate.

What you think?
Write your opinion on it.

Topic 42 : How To Take Care Of Our Elders ?

In past, there were no trained professionals to take care of the elderly people so, from the very beginning, most of the civilisation adopted a tradition in which younger people take care of their elderly parents. This type of behaviours is also found in another life forms.

Old age is an inevitable part of human beings. Everyone will be in that phase of life. It becomes a lot easier if someone is there to help out. If our younger children are with us at this time then life becomes a lot easier. The love and warmth of a family make it a memorable experience of life. Also, it is a good opportunity for the younger generation to learn from the experience of their elders. It is a self-sustaining cycle in which younger people take care of their elders and when they become old at that time children take care of them.

Nowadays, the world is changing and most of the people are working throughout the day and are having a very busy lifestyle so hiring a trained professional to take care of elderly ones is a good option. The trained professionals can take care of them and in case of any health issue, they provide proper medication. Also, it can help younger people to be focused on their work.

Overall, modern lifestyle and new emerging facilities have given the option to design one's life in a way he/she wishes. Nowadays older people are more active and take part in lots of activities which help them to stay happy and fit.

What you think?
Write your opinion on it.

Topic 43 : Role Of Younger And Older People In Growth Of A Nation

Among the three phases of life, young age is more energetic and dextrous. Young adults are having an important role in the development of the country. Young adults increase the pride of a country by winning a gold medal in sports activities. In another perspective, older people are having more experience. Older people also help to maintain unity in society.

Youth are more skilful and dextrous than any other section of the society. For example, younger people are more productive. Most of the private companies and other government services provide a good opportunity for them. Also, young people are more active in sports and other activities. They bring glory to the nation by winning a medal in different international competitions. The economy of any country is dependent on the working youth. They play an important role in the development of a country.

On the other hand, older people are having more experience. Older people maintain unity in society. For example, everyone respects the older member in his/her family. So, they resolve disputes and maintain unity in the family. Thus, the wisdom of older people is necessary to maintain peace in the country.

In conclusion, there are lots of benefits to the country having more young adults then that of other age group.

What you think?
Write your opinion on it.

Topic 44 : Working After Retirement

compared to the past, nowadays there are lots of medical facilities available in the market and due to all this advancement in medical technology, overall life expectancy has increased. This overall improvement in the quality of life can help a person to work in his/her old age. On the other hand, working in retirement can create an unnecessary burden on one's head.

The scheme of retirement was introduced by considering the fact that with ageing people become less dextrous and undergo decline in health. Nowadays with the advancement in medical technology the overall quality and standard of living has improved. This means that a person can work efficiently in his/her old age. Also, some jobs require more experience so people working in their old age are having more experience and they can perform better than the other inexperience people.

The more people working in their old age can lead to a decrease in the overall employment opportunities. Also, most of the people work throughout their life and save money so that they can pursue their hobbies or can spend on travelling, so doing work even after their retirement can lead to disappointment.

In short, people continuing their work after their retirement are always an asset and it can help the overall development of a country but there are few downsides of it.

What you think?
Write your opinion on it.

Topic 45 : Rise In Number Of Old People

The ratio of older people is increasing in many countries. This trend is having its own advantages and disadvantages. Older people are wise. They provide good leadership. Also, older people are very good at helping children. If the ratio of older people is increasing then it means that the overall life expectancy is increasing. On the other side, if the ratio of older people is increasing then there will be fewer children and younger people. Nation will have a shortage of skilful and fit employees.

The ratio of older people is increasing in many nations. It shows that the overall life expectancy of a human being is increasing. Older people have a good experience. There is always a requirement of an experienced person in each and every field. Also, older people are good at taking care of children. They read books to children and play with them. It really helps in the development of children.

On the other side, if the ratio of older people is increasing then there will be fewer children and younger people. It creates an imbalance in the society and nation have to face lots of problems. Nation will have a shortage of skilful employees. For example, Japan is one of the countries with a high ratio of older people. Japan is facing the problem such as lack of young employees and workers. Japan has to bring students and workers from other countries.

All in all, the ratio of older people must be balanced. Too many or too fewer old people can create lots of problems for the nation.

What you think?
Write your opinion on it.

Topic 46 : Is Increasing Trend In Production of Consumer Goods Is Damaging Environment ?

The products such as gadgets, computer/laptops, polythene and other plastic bags, toys and other accessories are in demand. The increase in population and the standard of living give rise to the demand and production of the above-mentioned goods.

The electronic gadgets and other appliances are made from silicon and other materials. The production of these devices requires lots of energy and other natural resources. With the rise in the demand for electronic devices lead to the consumption of more energy and limited natural resources. Also, the e-waste produced from these used electronic devices pollutes the environment. Thus, the rise in the demand for electronic devices lead us to more consumption of limited natural resources and left us with the harmful electronic wastes.

The other big concern is the rise in the demand for plastic and its derivatives. The plastic and other polythene bags are not decomposed so it is hard to manage the plastic waste. Also, some study shows that plastic is harmful to our health and hygiene.

The possible solution to the rise in the demand of consumer goods is recycled electronic devices and plastics. The refurbished electronic devices can help to reduce the production of new electronic devices and can satisfy the rising consumer demands. In the case of plastic, other material can be used which can be decomposable and cause no threat to the environment.

What you think?
Write your opinion on it.

Topic 47 : Is Cleanliness is Responsibility Of An Individual Or Government ?

Cleanliness is very important for inhibiting the spread of diseases. Resident must be health conscious and must take proper steps for disposal of garbage and maintaining cleanliness in their area. All people of society must voluntarily take part in cleaning and other activities for the betterment of their area. Contrary, as all the member of society have limited resources and are less organized than that of government so the government must take charge of cleaning and improve the different area of town. Government is more organized and have more resources for the proper disposal of garbage.

If garbage is accumulated at one place and if it is not properly disposed then there are chances of spread of harmful diseases. Citizens must be conscious of their health and hygiene. They must volunteer to take part in cleaning and organizing their area. They must plant trees and must maintain it by providing water and protection. The plantation provides fresh air and it reduces air pollution.

Contrary, common people have limited resources and are less organized than that of government and ruling authority, so the government must take charge for proper disposal of garbage, the government have the power to purchase required resources for maintaining cleanliness in the town. They can effectively dispose garbage and maintain cleanliness.

To recapitulate, a citizen must be conscious about maintaining cleanliness and must cooperate with the existing government in maintaining cleanliness.

What you think?
Write your opinion on it.

Topic 48 : How To Preserve Environment ?

The environment is the biggest asset to the planet earth. No other planets in our solar system contain the environment in which life can survive. So, protection of the environment is very essential and it is our responsibility to protect the environment.

The main cause of environmental degradation is our attitude toward it. Most of the people take it for granted and causes a lot of harm to the environment. The rich flora and fauna of our planet are one of its kind and unique in entire milky way. Our careless attitude toward it can lead to the extinction of very rare species. Few people are really aware of it and they are working hard to protect and restore our environment. Industrial pollution affects the most and so the scientists are working on to find out ways that can help to reduce pollution.

There are some NGO (non-governmental organizations) that are working on to protect the environment but most of the people are not conscious about environment protection. For example, most of the people take part in a rally to spread awareness about environmental protection but they do not take any action to protect it.

The simple thing such as the use of unnecessary plastic bags or other nondegradable materials causes lots of harm to the environment so the solution is to take care of it and to become responsible. Planting a small tree can help a lot to restore the environment.

In conclusion, human activities affected the environment is the bitter truth but the small steps like planting a tree can help a lot to restore the environment.

What you think?
Write your opinion on it.

Topic 49 : How To Restore Global Climate Changes ?

The global climate changes are caused by pollution and environmental degradation. The rise in the level of carbon dioxide due to the combustion of crude oil is the prime factor in global climate change. Individual efforts such as the use of public transport, proper management of waste, especially electronic waste, appropriate use of natural resources can make a difference. On the other hand, few people believe that the ruling government and big factories can change a situation.

The individual efforts are important and it can help to restore the global climate change. An individual can prefer public transportation, cycle or electric bike instead of a car or other CO_2 emitting vehicles. It will help to reduce pollution. The level of carbon dioxide will decrease. This small effort can lead to a major change in the global climate. Also, a person can make a habit to use natural resources in a judicious manner.

On the other hand, big factories can change their policy to restore the global climate. They can lower their industrial waste. The government can enforce stiffen policy to lower industrial pollution.

In conclusion, climate change can be restored back to equilibrium if the proper step is taken by the ruling government as well as common people.

What you think?
Write your opinion on it.

Topic 50 : How To Control Industrial Pollution ?

The increase in pollution and a rise in industrial growth are the factors causing higher industrial pollution. The global warming caused by industrial pollution is one of the major problems. Collecting higher taxes from the industries causing higher pollution is one of the solutions. There are other opinions too to reduce the overall industrial pollution.

There are lots of factors that affect the overall rise in pollution. The contribution of industries is more in increasing pollution. The regulation of industrial pollution is mostly done by private companies and most of the time industrial pollution is not controlled properly which causes lots of harm to the river and air. The government has formed strict rules and imposed higher taxes on the industries causing higher pollution and it helps to control industrial pollution.

There are lots of cases in which industries are more focused on profit and give the least consideration to the pollution control. Also, taxes can reduce pollution but it cannot change the problem caused by pollution. So, to reduce or compensate for the harm caused by industrial pollution more and more trees can be planted around the industrial areas. Also, industries can invest in research projects to reduce overall pollution.

In short, collecting higher taxes can help to control industrial pollution but it is not the solution to the harm caused by industrial pollution.

What you think?
Write your opinion on it.

Topic 51 : How To Save Diverse Flora And Fauna Of Earth ?

Plants and animals are an important part of our ecosystem. Each and every species are dependent on each other. The decrease in plantation due to human activities causes a threat to the environment. Wildlife plays a major role in sustaining the ecosystem. Extinction of some animals can cause a threat to the environment.

The major cause of the extinction of animals is due to hunting. In past, royal families used to do hunting and it was their hobby. The activities become popular and lots of people started hunting. Hunting leads to a drastic decline in the animal species. The reason behind the decline in the plantation is deforestation. Due to the rise in population and increase in demand of general public, trees are cut to satisfy the need for fire, furniture, paper and another household uses. The other reason for the decline in the plantation is a forest fire which wipes out a huge number of trees.

To change the situation, steps such as strict laws for the preservation of endangered species and spreading public awareness about the preservation of endangered species can play an important role in saving biodiversity. Public awareness can be spread by organizing seminars and broadcasting T.V. advertisement.

All in all, diverse flora and fauna can be preserved by spreading awareness and implementing strict rules.

What you think?
Write your opinion on it.

Topic 52 : Is outer space exploration worthy ?

Outer space exploration is very important to understand lots of physical phenomena and theories of cosmology. Spending money on space discoveries can come handy in times of space calamities such as asteroid collision. Also understanding and analysing outer space can help to discover a new civilization. Space travel can become a reality for space enthusiast. On the other side, space discoveries come with huge risks. As it requires more money, which can be helpful in solving other environmental and global problems.

Outer space discoveries lead us to lots of breakthrough in science and technology. Nowadays, we are equipped with technology which can identify asteroid or any other materials approaching the earth. Also, we can track it's a trajectory to avoid space calamities such as asteroid collision. Space discovery can lead us to other civilization that might be evolving in a milky way. If space travel becomes a reality then it can generate lots of revenue and provide new means of exploration for space travellers.

The latest movie 'Mission Mangal' shows how important is space exploration and how much effort and work are required behind a successful space mission. You can also watch movies like Gravity, Martian and series of Star Wars and star trek. Also, there are lots of videos on YouTube about space missions such as Apollo.

On the other side, space discoveries are very risky. Inspite of taking all precaution, there are lots of cases in which the whole mission become unsuccessful due to minor malfunction. Also, money used for space discoveries can be utilized to solve other major problems such as global warming and environmental degradation. As these problems are becoming a major concern, a proper allocation of money and resources can help to solve it.

All in all, no doubt space discoveries require ample of money but it helps to develop technologies which can be helpful in time of global catastrophe such as asteroid collision. Also, the environmental problem of plastic waste disposal can be addressed by space exploration and existing space technologies.

What you think?
Write your opinion on it.

Topic 53 : Do Machine Can Replace Hand Made Work

In past, there were no machines so each and every person were dependent on manual work but with the industrial revolution and rise in new machines lead to automation. Nowadays most of the work are carried out by machines.

To acquire any skill or to achieve mastery in any work, lots of practice is required. For example, A community is famous for its handicraft work and they are making it since very long period of time. As it is passed on from generation to generation so skilful and artistic work requires a very long time to evolve. Any machine or equipment is unable to do that type of work so it is better to have a handmade handicraft work than that of machine manufactured work.

On the other hand, a few works require precision. For example, laser-based cutting is very precise. Also, some work is very risky such as mining in which there is a risk of life so it is better to use machines to reduce the risk. The use of machines is increasing in the industrial environment to increase productivity and overall profit. Also, people are more inclined toward monitoring or controlling the machines rather than doing work by themselves. So, machines and automation are dominating the industrial environment.

No doubt that the machines help us with lots of work and make it easier but the handmade or artistic work is hard to replace.

What you think?
Write your opinion on it.

Topic 54 : Available Natural Resources For Energy Requirement

Scientifically there are two types of energy resources available on earth, namely i) renewable and ii) non-renewable. The renewable resources contain oil, natural gases etc. And non-renewable resources such as solar, wind, hydropower, biofuel and hydrogen energy. The major problem is that non - renewable resources are limited and we must harness renewable resources in an economically profitable manner.

Presently, we are using oil and coal as major resources of energy generation. The problem with the generation of energy is that oil and coal are going to exhausted in the coming 50 years. Also, worldwide consumption of oil and coal is increasing drastically. This led to price rise. Also burning of oil and coal causes environmental problems such as air pollution and global warming. So non - renewable resources are the only solution to the present requirement.

For the future, there are lots of energy sources available such as generating energy from water, solar energy, nuclear energy etc. Experts and scientists are also looking outside of earth, in deep space to harness the abundant energy available in the universe.

What you think?
Write your opinion on it.

Topic 55 : Who Is More Popular Scientists Or Politicians ?

People working in the field such as science, social service or any other kind of work that requires leadership are having more influence on the world. There are lots of scientists that are well - known throughout the world due to their epoch-making discoveries. On the other hand, there are lots of politicians out there who are very popular due to work they do which directly affect the lives of common people.

The level of influence of any person depends on his/her work. The scientists are working on the things that affect each and every one throughout the world. For example, the discovery of electricity and other inventions have changed the world. The reason for the development of most countries is a good research background. Also, science is a subject of fascination and mysteries and when scientists solve that mysteries it changes the way we see the world. There are lots of shows and documentaries which reflects smartness of the truly genius scientists.

On the other hand, there is a group of people working on to solve public problems and to improve the overall standard of living. The politicians are having lots of influence throughout the world. The main reason for their popularity is that they are more frequently reflected on television and other media. Also, social service and other activities carried out by politicians affects the lives of lots of people.

All in all, whether he/she is a scientist or a politician the thing that makes him/her more influential is the work they do and the impact of their work.

What you think?
Write your opinion on it.

Topic 56 : The Dilemma Of Being Celebrity

Popularity comes with responsibility. Most of the film actor or sports person become famous due to its hard work and dedication. Popularity has lots of benefits such as financial, fan following, good facilities and other benefits.

Popularity is the outcome of our work in the field. Popular people have to maintain their fan following and they have to be up to date on their work in order to maintain their fame. Popular people are connected with social media. Social media helps them to maintain their profile and provide a platform to interact with their followers. Popular people get lots of love and gifts from their followers. It motivates them to do the best work in their field and increase their influence.

Popularity comes with responsibility. Most people follow their favourite actor, sportsperson, scientists, politician or any other famous personality. For example, a sportsperson is smoking or taking drugs then it can have a negative influence on their followers. So famous personalities have to take their action wisely. Also, famous people have to face the media reporters and they have to maintain good relation with them.

All in all, popularity has its own perks and pitfalls.

What you think?
Write your opinion on it.

Topic 57 : Which Is Better Live Concert Or Live Telecast ?

Watching a live performance is a totally different experience than that of watching it on television. Live performance is having its own vibe and the joy we feel from it is inexpressible. On the other hand, watching a show on television saves lots of money and the viewer can watch it from any location.

Live performances always give better experience. As most of the television provides 2D or 3D information but live performance gives a real-life experience. Live performance also gives freedom to the spectator to look at wherever they want. Also, people can record or capture a photo of the best moment and can have a memorable experience.

There are also benefits of watching a show on television. It can save money. For example, the live concert is in New York then, first of all, there will be some expenses for travelling to New York and the amount of ticket will cost further. Also, a person can watch any concert on television without any noise or disturbance as most of the concert is noisy.

In short, there are some benefits to watching a show on television but it is always a memorable experience to be part of any live concert.

What you think?
Write your opinion on it.

Topic 58 : Is T.V. Advertisements Are Beneficial

T.V. (television) advertisement is a modern means of promotion. It helps to promote new prodducts and to expand a business. A good advertisement creates a long-lasting impression. It can be used to spread awareness about social problems. On the other hand, children are vulnerable and T.V. advertisement can easily manipulate them. Also, some T.V. advertisements show false information to increase their selling.

T.V. advertisements are created to draw in customers. The main purpose of T.V. advertisement is to promote their product. It helps to expand their business. Nowadays the advanced technologies help to create interesting advertisements. It is an important source to communicate with people. Some advertisements such as polio awareness, consumer rights are really helpful to spread awareness.

Lots of people get exploited by T.V. advertisements. Mostly children are vulnerable to T.V. advertisements. They easily get attracted by items shown in the advertisement. For example, children are easily attracted by T.V. advertisement of chocolates and spend lots of money on it, eventually they develop habit of eating excessive chocolates which lead to tooth decay.

In conclusion, advertisement is an important means of promoting products but sometimes it can lead to unexpected activities.

What you think?
Write your opinion on it.

Topic 59 : How To Utilize Materials More Effectively ?

The money spend on cosmetics is much more than that of other sectors such as food, shelter and other necessary resources. Due to the development of science, there are lots of cosmetic product available in the market. These products played an important role in the establishment of cosmetic industries. On the other hand, poor people are in the need of food and shelter. So, some part of the money must be utilized in the development of poor people.

Poverty is a major problem in most of the nation. Lots of people live in raw houses and streets. Some people even find it difficult to earn a two-time meal. So, the money spent on cosmetic and other beauty products can be utilized in providing a better shelter and food facility to the poor and needy people.

The cosmetic industry generates lots of employment and revenue. The cosmetic and other beauty product help to provide employment. Also, it helps the Bollywood industry to generate revenue. The celebrity is the main consumer of beauty products. So, it helps to provide employment and to generate revenue.

All in all, cosmetics and other beauty product must be used and manufactured efficiently and money must be spent on the development of poor and needy people.

What you think?
Write your opinion on it.

Topic 60 : Smartphones Are Advantageous Or Disadvantageous

The development of the modern era leads to lots of technological innovation. The most popular among it is the cell phone. The cell phone brought a new revolution. Nowadays people can't imagine their life without a cell phone.

Although the cell phone is having lots of features and applications, it is harmful to children. Cell phones easily grab the attention of children and they easily become fond of it which really hampers their overall growth. The children who spend most of their free - time playing games on a cell phone are the ones who misses the other essential sports activities. Children become more addicted to cell phone and it affects their study. There are more chances that children can misplace the cell phone.

The cell phone can become a boon for children at a time of emergency. For example, in the case of an accident or any other critical situation, a cell phone can be very helpful. Also, the cell phone can help to improve the critical thinking of children. As the world is moving towards technological advancement, it is better if children learn to use it from their childhood.

In conclusion, the good use of cell phones can help children but as childhood is about playing games with friends and learning new things it is always advisable to avoid excessive use of cell phones.

What you think?
Write your opinion on it.

___

Topic 61 : The Mystery Of Happiness

Economic development has brought us at a place where we relate our happiness and sorrow to our financial status. Money provides us the power to purchase the things that give us happiness. Also, there is a wide difference in the index of happiness between rich and poor people. Relating money to our happiness has downsides. In reality, personal satisfaction is utmost important in deciding our level of happiness. Also, research has shown that we get more happiness from travelling and exploring new places.

In the past few decades after the world wars ended, the world becomes more prosperous and this led to huge economic development. Nowadays we relate most of our happiness to our financial status. Money gives us the power to purchase things that make us happy. For example, we can purchase a projector and music system and can enjoy our favourite movies and television shows.

There is also the downside of relating money to happiness. We see a huge difference between rich and poor people. There are rich people who are unhappy and there are poor people who are happy. In reality, personal satisfaction is utmost important in deciding our level of happiness. Also, research has shown that we get more happiness from indirect things such as travelling, shopping, learning new things and exploring the new art forms. All these activities create a new connection in our brain which makes us happy.

To recapitulate, money gives us the power to purchase things which make us happy but our true happiness depends on our level of satisfaction, it has nothing to do with money or our financial status.

What you think?
Write your opinion on it.

Topic 62 : Requirement Of Security In Modern World

The development of science and technology have brought lots of change in the existing society. Nowadays the living standard of people is increased. They keep lots of gadgets and other expensive objects in their house. This brings the threat of security. Robbery and other crimes are increased with the development of mankind. To protect all the gadgets and other accessories proper security measures are to be implemented.

The development of human race and increase in valuables has raised the concern of security. The means such as CCTV camera and lockers are helpful in providing security. It provides protection and helps to keep an eye on the expensive objects. The security measure also provides extra benefits such as remote monitoring. Due to this feature, we can keep an eye on the expensive objects remotely. Also, watchmen are kept for security to ensure the security of the whole house.

There are few drawbacks of security in urban areas. People feel vulnerable and exposed due to security measures. People have to spend more money on purchasing instruments for security purpose.

All in all, security measures provide lots of benefits which outweigh its disadvantages.

What you think?
Write your opinion on it.

Topic 63 : How To Reduce Wastage Of Food ?

Presently, we are having lots of option for food. New shops and restaurant are opening. This development in the food industry provides cheap food with tempting offers. Also, lots of people have a habit of ordering more food than that of requirement. The possible solution is to strictly regulate the licence of new food shops and restaurants. Also, regular food quality inspection can help to decrease food wastage. People must be encouraged to order food as per their requirement and to decrease the waste of food. The leftover food can be supplied to needy people with the help of NGO.

The recent development in food leftover industry leads to the opening of lots of new food shops and restaurants. Due to increasing competition, food shops and restaurants are providing cheap food with tempting offers. People are now habituated to order more food than that of requirement. It creates a lot of food wastage.

To solve this problem the strict regulation of licence for new restaurants and food shops must be implemented. Regular food quality inspection is very helpful in improving food quality and decreasing food wastage. Food quality inspection can control the wastage of food by helping food shops and restaurants in improving food quality and henceforth increasing food price and decreasing food wastage. People must be encouraged to order food as per their requirement to decrease food wastage. Also, leftover food must be supplied to needy people with the help of non-government organizations.

To recapitulate, the development of the food industry and food habits are responsible for food wastage. Food wastage can be decreased by strictly administering the licence of food shops and restaurants.

What you think?
Write your opinion on it.

Topic 64 : Is It A Good Idea To Explore About Different Cultures ?

Due to geographical partition and man-made borders, we evolved with different culture and a wide range of traditional history. Learning the country's own history and culture is basic human nature. It helps to connect with our nation and motivates us to take part in the development of our nation. On the other hand, due to technological advancements and other scientific developments, we are a part of the global community. Understanding and learning global history and culture help us to form a global perspective. It also helps to explore different parts of the world.

From the very childhood, we start to learn our own culture and traditions. It helps us to connect with our community by celebrating festivals, learning new art forms. By understanding the history of our country, we can learn moral values and essential skills which can help us to form our personality. By knowing our rich heritage and culture we can feel prideful and it helps to develop a sense of unity among us.

Simultaneously, we must also learn about global history and other cultures. Day by day we are becoming a part of a globally connected community because of rapid development in technologies and another scientific breakthrough. Also, information about foreign culture and history can help to explore a different part of the world. During travelling to other countries, the most important is to know about the common language and if we have information about local history then it makes our experience more joyful.

To recapitulate, learning local history and our nation's tradition and culture is a primary thing but understanding the global history and different cultures can help to shape our perception and personality.

What you think?
Write your opinion on it.

Topic 65 : Impact Of Young People Migrating To Urban Areas

People living in rural areas are having very fewer opportunities compared to one living in urban areas. So, they travel to urban areas to find more resources to study and work. It has both pros and cons. They get good opportunities to work and study in urban areas. Cities are having well- equipped schools and colleges. Also, it contains lots of job opportunities. In return, they have to leave the pollution-free environment of rural areas and have to live in concrete buildings away from their family members.

The migration of people from rural to an urban area leads to the development of cities. Industries and business are the backbone of developing cities. It requires skilled people to carry out work. The people coming from a rural area play a major role in the development of their industries and other business. Contrary, cities require more space to accommodate migrated people and it increases the population of cities. This led to slum areas and congested housing. Also, it leads to the threat of overexploitation of resources of cities.

The advantages of rural to urban migration are the development of countries economy. It helps to increase the life-style of people, it increases the overall literacy rate of the country. Contrary, there few disadvantages such as an increase in the population of cities, overexploitation of resources which can be managed by proper city management.

In conclusion, rural to urban migration is having its own perk and pitfall but it is the demand of the modern world.

What you think?
Write your opinion on it.

Topic 66 : Urban Migration And Its Effects

Food, clothes and adobe are the three main requirements of human beings. Due to urbanization, most of the farmers travel to urban areas. It hampers the production of agricultural goods. There are lots of uncertainty in agriculture as it depends on rain and other resources. Also, the farmer has to do a large investment in it. It can be solved by improving agricultural facilities and providing financial aid to farmers.

Farmers have to deal with lots of problems such as drought and arrangement of resources. As farming depends on factors such as the availability of rain and other resources. They face the problem in gaining profit. Also, farming is a very hard task and it requires lots of manpower. So, most of the farmer give up farming and go to urban cities to get employment. There is a huge difference in the lifestyle of the village and cities. Which attracts farmer for migration.

The solution is to provide financial aid to farmers. Farmers can be encouraged to use advanced technologies such as tractors, advanced ploughing machines and pesticides to increase agricultural production. Also improving the lifestyle of the village can motivate the farmer to stay in town.

All in all, farming is a hard task but by providing financial aid and other resources we can encourage farmer to do effective farming.

What you think?
Write your opinion on it.

Topic 67 : Pros And Cons Of International Tourism

International tourism brings prosperity in the life of local people. It also helps to develop the economy of a developing country. Further, International tourism helps to develop a good relationship between the two nations. On the other hand, international tourism causes environmental problems. Also due to international tourism, there is a risk of spreading of infectious diseases.

International tourism must be increased in a developing country. It provides an opportunity for local people and vendors to carry out business. International tourism helps to develop the economy of a developing country by increasing trade and commerce. International tourism provides an opportunity for people to explore different parts of the world. Also, an anthropologist can carry out research on a different ancient culture and their heritage. Local people can also learn about new culture and heritage. International tourism also helps to develop a good relationship between the two countries.

International tourism causes environmental problems. As tourist travel to different countries, they create waste. So, a proper waste management system must be established. Also, there are chances of spread of viral diseases. There are few tourists who harm historical places by inscribing their names on walls.

All in all, international tourisms have lots of advantages compared to the disadvantages.

What you think?
Write your opinion on it.

Topic 68 : Nowadays travelling Abroad Is Easier

Travelling is always being a popular activity among people. Travelling has lots of benefits. It helps to explore different monuments and cultures. Also, travelling is a major source of revenue generation in developing countries. Further, travelling is becoming cheaper due to development in new means of transportation. All together there is an increase in international tourism. Travelling come with few negative consequences. It increases pollution and garbage. International tourism is having a small risk too such as plane crash and other accidents.

Travelling, especially international travelling has ample of benefits. It provides an opportunity for people to explore different cultures and their heritage. It also helps to increase the economic condition of developing countries. International travelling creates a friendly atmosphere among developing and developed nations. It also helps anthropologist and other researchers to explore different parts of the world and carry out their research studies.

Everything comes with favourable and unfavourable conditions, so does the travelling. International travelling creates pollution and garbage. As travellers migrate from one place to another, there is a risk of a plane crash and other accidents. Also, if a traveller is suffering from viral disease then there is a risk of spread of disease from one continent to another.

All in all, international travelling has ample of benefits, if proper steps are taken ensure safe international travelling.

What you think?
Write your opinion on it.

Whole universe is dark but still there are some self-luminous things like sun and other stars. Our soul is also a self-luminous body so never let it fade away in this dark universe.

"Darkness of the universe is an opportunity for the stars to shine"

www.ingramcontent.com/pod-product-compliance
Ingram Content Group UK Ltd.
Pitfield, Milton Keynes, MK11 3LW, UK
UKHW042002230426
12048UKWH00009B/488